PAGE *from a* TENNESSEE JOURNAL

PAGE *from a* TENNESSEE JOURNAL

FRANCINE THOMAS HOWARD

PUBLISHED BY

 amazonencore

PRODUCED BY

MELCHER MEDIA

Text copyright © 2010 Francine T. Howard

Printed in the United States of America
10 11 12 13 14 15 16 / 10 9 8 7 6 5 4 3 2 1

Published by AmazonEncore
P.O. Box 400818
Las Vegas, NV 89140

Produced by Melcher Media, Inc.
124 West 13th Street
New York, NY 10011
www.melcher.com

Library of Congress Cataloging-in-Publication Data
2009913661
ISBN-13: 978-0-98255-506-4
ISBN-10: 0-9825550-6-7

Jacket design by Laura Klynstra
Interior design by Jessi Rymill
Cover photographs: (top) © Vintage Collection/arcangel-images.com;
(bottom left) © Natural History Museum of London/Alamy;
(bottom right) courtesy of the Library of Congress

SUSTAINABLE FORESTRY INITIATIVE

Certified Chain of Custody
Promoting Sustainable
Forest Management
www.sfiprogram.org

Melcher Media strives to use environmentally responsible suppliers
and materials whenever possible in the production of its books.
For this book, that includes the use of SFI-certified interior paper stock.

SOMETIMES I THINK YOU WHISPERED YOUR SECRET
INTO MY EARS WHEN I WAS STILL IN MY CRIB
BECAUSE YOU COULDN'T TELL ANYONE ELSE.
I PRAY THAT I'VE DONE YOU JUSTICE.

Thank you, Miz Mabry.

CHAPTER ONE

Annalaura Welles stirred out of her fitful sleep to the certainty of two things. Husband John was gone for good this time, and even with the help of her four young children, she would be unable to bring in the tobacco harvest by the end of August. Though this was coming up the second year she'd sharecropped the McNaughton mid-forty, she still wasn't used to living in the converted upper reaches of a barn.

The sky loomed dark through the small window cut at the foot of her sleeping alcove. She owned no clock, but her tired bones told her it was about a half-hour 'til sun rising, and she laid a tentative hand on daughter Lottie's bobtailed braids as the five-year-old slept soundly beside her. Almost drowning out the child's soft sighs were the snorts of the three pigs on the bottom level, fifteen feet below. The smell of their fresh dung made its way up through the openings in the floorboards. The cows hadn't lowed their own good mornings yet, and she wanted her Cleveland to get a little more rest.

She had to work him like a man, but Annalaura was always mindful that her oldest boy was not yet twelve years old. She fretted just as much over Doug and little Henry. All four of her children would have to step into the world way too soon if she couldn't sort out this mess John had left her. A moonbeam flooded through the open crack in the roof that McNaughton had neglected to repair during last winter's snows and she realized she had awakened too early again.

The first two weeks after John left in early June hadn't been too bad.

She knew going into her wedding thirteen years ago that no man as good-looking as John Welles was going to stay faithful for long to a woman plain as a corn-bread skillet. But now it was mid-August with harvest time closer than she wanted. In all his wanderings, John had never been away from her, or his children, more than two weeks. She reached an arm over her head to locate the splintery rafter beam to guide her as she eased herself to sitting. She had knocked herself in the head too many times to attempt getting up quickly in these tight quarters. She knew colored still lived in some bad conditions in Tennessee, but after all, this was Our Lord's year of 1913. Even in slavery times, her Aunt Becky and her own grandma Charity had lived better than this.

She shifted her feet onto the rough, knot-pitted floorboards and raised her body upright with just the merest rustling of the corn husks that made up the mattress John had given her as a wedding gift. Before she stood, she checked again on Lottie, who had barely stirred in her sleep. Annalaura had no intention of awakening her children before sunup, knowing they would get no rest and precious little food until way past sundown. Lottie had squirmed most of the night in the heat of the barn. Sometimes Annalaura could swear that the pigs and the cows below were choking all the air out of her children for their own breathing. Standing, she bunched her nightdress in her hand. The thin fabric felt wringing-wet damp with her sweat. Barefoot and stepping carefully from the planked box McNaughton had built to serve as a bed for his tenant farmers, she avoided all the familiar squeaks and creaks in the wide-apart floorboards as she checked on the remnants of last night's supper, which would soon serve as today's breakfast. Annalaura lifted the cracked saucer she'd laid over the remains to ward off the mosquitoes and the mice. She poked at the four hardened biscuits. Though her three-year-old, Henry, had reached for a second, she had to take the crusty bread from his hand and divide it between her two older boys. No amount of explaining that she had flour enough for only ten biscuits a day, and that had to serve the five of them for two meals, could comfort a wailing Henry.

As she walked across the floor to the clothes nail hanging on the wall above middle son Doug and baby Henry's little pallet of a bed, she remembered how John had described the place when he first saw it. "This room ain't big enough to hold three six-foot-high men laid head to foot in either direction." Then, she had to laugh to keep from crying at how low they lived. Now she was terrified that soon even this sty of a place wouldn't be theirs.

In the dimness, Annalaura shimmied her nightdress over her hips and reached for the nail that held her work outfit. As she lifted the gown over her head, her hand brushed her breast. For a second she wondered what John would think of her body now. He had always pretended that her middling height frame was "just right … not beanpole skinny nor so fat your bottom fill up two seats on the church pew."

With food being stretched like it was, Annalaura knew she had lost weight. She put a quick hand underneath her breast and gave it a little boost. Hadn't changed all that much she thought. Her husband had told her that she had tight tits, and she guessed that was still so. Sometimes, when he didn't know she was watching, she'd catch a gleam in his eye like he believed she had the best-looking female shape in all of Montgomery County. But what did she care what John Welles thought about her body? She couldn't put any stock in the words of a man who had probably laid down with a dozen women before he ever met her and two dozen afterward.

Annalaura reached for her work shirt with its two missing top buttons. Waiting to earn enough money for a new spool of thread, she had saved them in the old snuff tin she'd believed she had hidden so well in the smoke house. Never mind, she thought, as she stepped into her ankle-slapping skirt, the waist band twisting on her narrowed body. There'd be no one who mattered to see that her blouse wasn't properly fastened under her chin. She patted her chemise and drawers, which lay on the shelf above the nail hooks. She only had one set, and they were for Sunday. Besides, there was no need to put on drawers and a chemise on a scorcher of an August day like this one promised to be. Not when she would be in the fields from just past breakfast 'til sunset. With her work brogans laced on her feet, Annalaura climbed down the ladder leading to the bottom floor, hitching up her skirt as she moved. She held her breath as she walked by the three sows and the two milk cows. She didn't know why. They were no more smelly when she stood close to them than they were when they sent their special aromas drifting upward to the barn rafters and her family.

Several feet outside the barn sat the chicken coop. Just beyond, stood the brick smoke house that McNaughton allowed the family to use for the preparation of its meals. That is, when Annalaura had food enough to prepare a meal. Inside the makeshift kitchen, Annalaura checked the larder. With half a barrel of flour left, she figured she had enough to last 'til the harvest in mid-September. She had a jar of dried butter beans, and used with care, the contents could be stretched into next month. The only slab of bacon John left her had run out two weeks ago, but she still had half a can of bacon fat. The cornmeal was low, but she reckoned she had enough of that for bread once a week 'til harvest. The garden had very little left in it. A few pinched-in tomatoes, one row of tired green onions, and the last of the pole beans were all that were left standing. In normal times, she would have put in the turnips and her other fall vegetables, but there had been no money for the seed—not after John had cleaned out her snuff tin of all but two dollars back in June. She hefted the weight of the salt container and the baking soda. Both were too light to the touch. Annalaura had been taught to be a good manager, and she suspected that was the real reason John Welles picked her over all those other females who swarmed over him like a hog going to slop.

She had been seventeen when twenty-two-year-old John came parading his wares in front of her. To say that she was surprised was to put the lie to the sun coming up in the east. Yet, when he asked, she had nodded her slow yes. Even back then she wasn't really sure about John as a husband, and now she had the hard times to back up her earlier doubt.

To announce the arrival of the sun, the rooster began strutting his stuff and greeted the day with a piercing crow. The dark silhouettes of the tobacco plants came marching up at her like short children. And that was the problem. Would the plants be tall enough for harvest in two weeks?

As much as she wanted, she couldn't put off facing the truth much longer. She carried a pat of lard for the breakfast biscuits as she climbed back up the ladder. The cows mooed their discomfort.

"Ma, I can start the fire in the smoke house." Cleveland's voice came out of the gloom of the second platform bed on the opposite side of their living space.

Annalaura stepped off the top rung to see young Henry stretched out on the straw pallet he shared with Doug. Lottie had already climbed down from their platform bed to sit herself on one of the two backless crates at the table.

"Never you mind, Cleveland, I put the fire on. Lottie, I put some butter beans on the back of the stove for supper. I want you to watch them." Annalaura set the chipped cup with the bacon drippings on the table. Little Henry jumped from his perch and raced his middle brother, Doug, for the same crate chair. Doug won, and Henry set up a howl.

"Come sit with me, Henry, and hush up that noise. Cleveland and Doug, we've got a hard day ahead of us."

"Momma, cain't we have somethin' else besides biscuits and bacon fat for breakfast?" Lottie dropped her head on the table for an instant. Brightening, the five-year old's cocoa-brown face broke into a wide grin. "Let's have eggs. I'll go fetch them." The little girl thundered to the ladder.

Annalaura shook her head.

"Doug will help you put them on to boil, but they ain't fo' breakfast. They gonna be our noonday dinner." She reached for one of Henry's shoes and tried to jam his foot into the tight-fitting high top.

"Momma, I'm hungry now. I want eggs now." Lottie poked out her lower lip and gave Annalaura her best "po' chile" pout.

"Eggs now. Eggs now." Henry clapped his hands. The grin spread over his face as he celebrated his sister's misery.

"Hush up, both of you." It pained Annalaura to let her voice sound as sharp as it did. Too roughly, she shoved the shoe onto Henry's protesting foot. Ignoring his screams as best she could, she eased him to the floor as she tried to compose herself. Annalaura couldn't let the children see how bad off things really were. At least, not until she could come up with a plan. She got her voice under control. "No mo' than four eggs now. I don't think them old hens is laying much any mo'."

"Then, can we have that old one for supper tonight? Ain't had chicken in ever so long." Doug's voice sounded chipper, though at nine, he should already have known the answer.

If not, Cleveland was there to supply it to him.

"No, you jackass. If we keep eatin' the laying hens, we won't have no eggs at all." Cleveland dodged Doug's slap at his head only to be met by Annalaura's backhand to his shoulder.

"Ain't I told you 'bout no swearin'? 'Specially in front of ladies and children." Annalaura looked down at Henry, still on the ground protesting the offending shoes.

"Papa swears sometimes." Cleveland folded his arms across his chest and wagged his head, looking so much like John that it gave Annalaura a startle.

"Your papa ain't never swore at me nor you children not nary a time and you know it. Decent folks don't use those kind of words." Annalaura clamped her eyes shut for an instant as her head swirled her world around her. She couldn't take out her fear on her children. "It's just a hard day comin' up, is all." She watched her eldest drop his hands to the table and look over at her.

"Every day is hard for us, Momma." Cleveland's voice dripped the sound of a weary old man.

Annalaura sucked in her lip. It wasn't right for children to have to pay for the sins of the father. While Henry bellowed his discomfort and Doug and Lottie scampered down the ladder, Annalaura stood to get the kitchen knife. It was time to cut the sole from the leather on Henry's shoes. Cleveland followed her with his eyes.

"You think Papa will be back befo' the harvest?" For all his manly cares, there was still something of the little boy in her firstborn, and Annalaura was glad that all his childhood hadn't been taken from him. He still had hope.

"Yo' papa be back in due time. He left us here 'cause he knew we'd be all right." She pulled off the vexing shoes. Annalaura didn't like telling lies to her children, but she had just come upon the idea herself that her husband was gone for good.

"You think Papa's gone to Clarksville?" Cleveland's doubting voice showed more than budding growing-up lows and highs.

"Clarksville's not but five miles away." Annalaura knew that if John were in that close-knit colored community, she would surely know about it. "I reckon you could be right. Yo' papa's sure to walk through that do' just about any time now." With the shoe sliced open to allow Henry's toes wiggle room, she swept the boy back onto her lap.

As Annalaura slipped the shoes onto her toddler's feet, Lottie and Doug bounded up the top rung of the ladder.

"Did you get them cows milked, Doug?" She sat a now-pacified Henry back on the floor as Cleveland headed down the ladder.

"Ain't much milk, Momma." Doug held out the half-full pail of still foamy white liquid. Henry grabbed a cracked cup from the table and banged its side.

"Why'd old man McNaughton take that calf last month, Momma?" Doug asked.

"Ain't nobody know the ways of white folks. I heard tell he sold it." She guided Henry's hand into the pail and helped him fill his mug to brimming.

Lottie, grabbing the only other cup the family owned, dipped it into the bucket, splashing a few drops of milk onto Henry's face. Doug stood staring with unseeing eyes at the two young ones. Annalaura scowled. Her Doug was not a patient child.

"Lottie, let Doug have a sip of yo' milk," she commanded a protesting Lottie.

Her second son looked up at her, one bare foot behind the opposite knee.

"Momma, you think I can go to school after harvest?" Doug looked back at her with the face she thought looked most like her own.

They shared the same copper-shaded brown skin and the same wide-set amber-colored eyes. She didn't know how to answer this brightest of her children.

"You said I could go to school when the tobacco got in."

"Lord, boy. Why are you botherin' me with school? We got us nothin' but work aplenty to get that tobacco in." She put an extra sharp edge to her words to hide her own growing misery. She'd find a way to fix this mess. She always had.

"I got to go to school after last harvest. Didn't have to quit 'til spring plowin' neither." Defiance crept into her boy's voice, and she knew what was coming next. "Papa would let me go."

Annalaura dug her nails into her palms to keep from screaming out the truth to this child. "Get yo' boots on and get on out to the field. If we can get this tobacco sticked by September, I'll make sure yo' papa lets you go to school."

The smile on her boy's face was worth the lie.

CHAPTER TWO

Alexander McNaughton looked over the food wife Eula Mae spread before him. It was the same breakfast she had prepared nearly every day of their twenty-year marriage. His eyes swept over the green, flower-printed oilcloth covering the kitchen table. Everything looked like it was there. A mess of eggs—she usually scrambled four for him—the four thick slices of bacon cut from the slab kept in the smoke house, the porridge bowl brimming to the top with grits, the potatoes cut into chunks and cooked in lard, the basket of fresh-baked biscuits in the center of the table, his big mug of black coffee were all there. Yet, something was missing. He glanced over at Eula standing at the stove tossing the tops of the green onions into the grease sizzling in the big cast-iron skillet. He watched her finish off the second helping of potatoes she knows he will want. Without a look in his direction that he could detect, Alex watched his wife pick up the crock of butter, turn, and walk toward him. She set the butter down on the table within easy reach. He gave her a barely perceptible nod as he picked up his fork.

Eula was good that way. Alex didn't have to waste time telling her the same things over and over. She just knew what had to be done around the place and got right to it. Unlike most women, Eula didn't spend her time yammering over nothing. If it hadn't been for the rare, late delivery of the butter this morning, Alexander wouldn't have given his wife even this much considering. Sometimes, a thought entered his head that he should tell Eula how much she meant to him, but loving words had never come easy for him. Besides, speeches full of sugar could turn a good woman's head and spoil her. He shot a second quick glance at his wife. What Eula lacked in looks, she more than made up for in hard work. With her tall, sturdy frame and arms almost as big around as his own, Alex never doubted that he had chosen the right woman all those years ago.

Not that he had much choice, mind you. Lawnover never did have a belle in all the forty-three years of his life. The closest claim to a beauty came from the neighboring Thornton place—Eula's younger sister, Bessie. Now, that girl had potential. Much smaller-framed than Eula, with high, pointed tits, and hair the color of corn tassels, Alex had thought about sparking her even though the Thornton clan stood more than two notches above his own in what passed for Lawnover society. But, before he could act, some rich dandy from Kentucky swept her away. With his hundred and sixty acres of hardscrabble tobacco land, Alex couldn't compare to a man with three hundred and sixty acres of good Kentucky bottom.

After Bessie Thornton, no respectable, single white women were left in Lawnover except for two widows, and they both had children. Alex did not fancy raising another man's get. Since his place had to be farmed, he needed a no-nonsense woman who didn't need a lot of petting or pretty words. He took his chances with Eula. Though she was a Thornton, her homely, round face and big-boned body had already made her a spinster. When her father said yes and Eula didn't object, they married.

Eula took her seat opposite him at the table just as Alex mopped up the last of the bacon grease with a biscuit. She set the fresh bowl of fried potatoes down. He signaled that he wanted no more. He spotted the look of mild surprise on her face.

"Got to go check on the mid-forty this morning." He was not in the habit of telling his wife his comings and goings but today was an especially busy one. "That friend of Ben Roy's is comin' by to leave the rest of the money for the calf. Tell him to put it on the bench in the smoke house."

Running his hand through his still thick, pale yellow hair, Alexander moved to his feet, sloshing a bit of coffee onto the table. He caught Eula looking at the top of his head. At least he hadn't gone bald like almost all of Eula Mae's male Thornton kin. As she wiped up his coffee spill with a clean dishrag, she worked her mouth to speak.

"Did I hear that the colored man on the mid-forty run off?" Eula didn't usually start a conversation with him.

Alex had already moved toward the door when he turned back to the sound of his wife's voice.

"Something like that." He took in her look as she worked her skinny lips to say something more.

Lucky for her that she had never been pretty because time hadn't done too much more damage except for the gray streaking her field-mouse-colored hair. Her sun-reddened skin had long ago taken on the look of badly tanned leather, pockmarked with pea-pod-size brown dots. Alex knew that was the way of it with white farm women.

"Isn't he the same colored man that brought in the big money last year on that po' piece of land you rented him?" She held her eyes at the collar of his shirt.

It didn't pain him much to give Eula her due when it came to managing the household money. There was none better in all of Lawnover, but no woman needed to know all of her husband's business. He didn't like discussing money with a woman, but Eula was right. He had let the sharecropper family farm his worst forty acres last year, and they had made him three thousand dollars, more than twice as much as any other tenant farmer he ever had, black or white.

"I remember when they come here asking to farm the place. The man…what was his name…he said he could make some money for you." Eula turned her eyes directly on him.

"I recollect him saying some words like that, but all niggers pretend they can bring in a bumper crop. You can't set no store by what a nigger says." Alex remembered the man. "Name of John, I recall. Said he was John Welles." Then, he remembered the woman. She was part of the colored family that had lived on Thornton land since way before the War of Secession.

"He looked strappin' big enough to do the job, and that oldest boy looked like he could be a pretty good help too." Eula looked him straight in the eye as she spoke. "Ben Roy says he hasn't seen him around in a month of Sundays." Eula walked back over to the sink and pumped water over the dirtied dishrag.

Alex frowned. Why was Eula's older brother meddling in his business?

"Ain't the first time that nigger's run off. Usually stays a week or two. I reckon I know the ways of my hands better than your brother." Alex glared at his wife. She knew as well as he that the tenant farmers were his business, not hers, and especially not Ben Roy Thornton's.

"It's just that I had a feeling early on about that man." She wrung out the dishcloth as she turned toward him, her eyes searching for a spot somewhere between his collar and chin. "Did it seem to you that the man was a bit too forward? Not uppity, mind you, just a little…" Eula's voice trailed down low.

Alex read respectful apology in both her words and her eyes. Though he had every right to be upset at his wife's indiscretion, he nodded his head. She was only a female. Even so, Eula did seem to have a good head for sorting out people. Most times, she had the good sense to know that it had to be the husband who decided these things. Still, there had been something about the sharecropper that caught Alex's eye two years ago. Maybe Eula was right. The fellow had skirted too close to uppity.

"It's not but two weeks 'til harvest." Eula's voice strained out of her throat. "If the man is gone, who you gonna get to bring in the tobacco?" The quick flash of worry that crossed his wife's face was dashed away almost before he could see it.

"I reckon I can sort that out without either you or Ben Roy telling me how," Alex snapped as he scowled his displeasure.

What had gotten into Eula? Had his wife talked around the barn to get to what was really bothering her—the tobacco harvest? Yes, it would hit him in the pocketbook in a tight year if the nigger actually had run off, but money worries were not for women. Eula knew that. Talk of money around any of the Thorntons always started that rumble in his stomach. Most of the time Alex felt just fine with the clothes, food, and furniture he'd provided for Eula in their twenty years together. But, every now and again, something came along to remind him that he had married a Thornton girl, raised with taffeta dresses, real china plates, and a half dozen colored cooks and maids. He'd never had a harvest big enough to provide his wife with even one full-time cleaning woman. Not that

Eula had complained about his ability to support her. At least, not that Alex had noticed.

Eula dropped her head and stared at the well-scrubbed floorboards. Both reddened hands went to her bosom. He watched her suck in and then poke out her lower lip like she wanted to say her sorrys. Instead, she walked to their black wood stove and stirred the peaches he finally sniffed bubbling in the big pot.

"You canning more preserves?" He tried to soften his criticism. Eula had meant no disrespect, he was certain. "I'll bring you back some mash, and you can make peach brandy."

Without looking behind him, he stepped out of the door. Alexander had to fix this mess on the mid-forty. He couldn't afford to lose three thousand dollars and a chance to get Eula a little help with the cleaning. If the man was really gone, he'd have to throw the woman and her get off the place and find another nigger soon.

CHAPTER THREE

At only ten in the morning the sun had already blazed through the long sleeves of Annalaura's shirt. Perspiration cascaded down her forehead and arms as she swung her hoe at the offending weeds. Standing upright, she wiped the sweat off her face as she glared at the trespassing foliage. The weeds were keeping the tobacco plants low. She lifted an arm again and planted it across her forehead, wishing that the threadbare cotton of her work shirt could sop up some of the sweat coming faster than she could wipe it away.

Annalaura tapped the hoe to the ground. 'Cropping had always been tough work, but last year, with John, Cleveland, and even Doug, the family had stayed on top of the job. Without John... she pushed the thought of her missing husband from her head. She glanced over at Henry, who had dropped to his knees in the next row. The child had mounded a pile of dirt scooped from around the rugged root of one weed. He wielded the stalk of a particularly low-growing tobacco plant to push a small pebble over his newly constructed "hill." The boy had given voice to each piece in his play.

"Henry," Annalaura shouted. "Stop that playactin', and get on up ahead to find me another patch of weeds." She watched a reluctant Henry stop his game.

Untying the bandanna from her head to wipe at more sweat, Annalaura sighted Lottie over her shoulder. She had assigned her daughter's weed-pulling duties close to the path that separated the barn and smoke house from the field. That way, Lottie could run in and check on the supper butter beans every hour or so. But Lottie was neither checking on supper nor pulling weeds. The girl skipped between two rows of tobacco, singing her made-up song. Annalaura shook her head. Unscrewing the lid from a Mason jar full of fresh drawn well water, she motioned Henry toward her. Seeing the water, the boy ran to his mother and reached for the container. Annalaura guided the rim to his lips. She called over her shoulder to Lottie without looking at her daughter.

"Stop that skippin'. Take yourself a draw of water and get on back to work." She nodded her head in the general direction of a second Mason jar laying on the ground near the smoke house.

With Henry squatting on the dirt watching the antics of an earthworm, Annalaura took a swig of liquid from her own jar. She wet her palm with a few drops and rubbed her hands over her cheeks. So much heat sprang from her legs that she felt they had been wrapped tight in a feather quilt. She flapped her long skirt to stir up a bit of air. The relief was short-lived. Sucking in her lower lip, she bent down and grabbed the back hem of her skirt. She brought the cloth forward through her legs and up to her waist. Annalaura snatched up the wide sides and tied the whole thing into a knot at her middle. While the briars might prick at her bare legs, at least from ankle to mid-thigh, her legs would get some relief from the suffocating skirt. Rolling up her shirtsleeves and flapping her arms in the air, Annalaura tried to stir up another breeze while her eyes scanned the acres for Cleveland. The boy was nowhere to be seen.

Ever since John disappeared, Cleveland had taken on the toughest jobs without being told. Annalaura reckoned he must have been working the fence line dividing McNaughton's mid-forty from his back acreage. She knew the tenant farmers on that piece had a better spot of land than she and John had been given to farm. At her colored church on Sunday mornings, she spotted the family as newcomers to Lawnover. While the woman was round and pudgy, the man was of good size and their two sons looked almost grown. The family hadn't said more than a polite "howdy do" to the old-time Lawnover colored. Still, even with all their back-forty hands, it had been the Welles family who brought in the most, and the best quality, tobacco of all the McNaughton acres last year.

The new family was on the back acres again this harvest. Like everyone else in Lawnover, they would know of her troubles. Annalaura realized they believed they could best the Welles family in 'cropping now that John was gone. She tried to swallow away a lump that came into her dry throat. If only she could say a good, out-loud cuss word against her missing husband. She shook the notion away. Annalaura didn't have the energy to waste on a man as stuck on himself as John Welles.

When the dandy of Lawnover came courting, nobody had been more surprised than she. Annalaura even told her Aunt Becky she wasn't sure about this caller. Didn't folks call him a "sportin' man?" But Becky said John had more than gambling, drinking, and woman-chasing in his head. With his good sense and fine looks, he was the colored catch of the county. Annalaura had never wanted a "catch." She just wanted a man who would work alongside her—a man who wanted more than to sharecrop some white man's acres for the rest of his life. John Welles was not only discontent to tenant farm, he also wasn't happy staying true to just one woman. Annalaura tossed her head to clear it. She had no more time for a man who would leave his wife and children in such a fix.

She dropped to a squat and pulled at a particularly bothersome weed. From her spot, she looked up at the sky to see nothing but an uncommon blue. Almost all the rest of Montgomery County was praying against rain this close to harvest, but not her. Annalaura needed those shoots to grow bigger, and she needed that spurt right away.

A twitch shot through the right side of her back. She unwound her knees and hips and arched herself to her feet. Raising her hands over her head to stretch out a threatening kink, she looked down at Henry. Still spread-legged on the ground some ten yards distant, the boy played both parts in a make-believe puppet show using two weeds to act out the parts. Annalaura shook her head. She had no further words for either of her youngsters. She could only drive them so far. As she swung around toward Lottie, two crows on the fence post separating the main lane from the rough path leading to the barn and smoke house took sudden flight. Annalaura shaded her eyes with a hand. Her heart did a two-step as she stared down the path at a horse and rider trotting toward the barn and her.

"Henry, get over here, now." She had no time to cajole her son with soft-sounding words. Even a three-year-old had to recognize the sound of danger in a mother's voice. Without moving her head as the rider approached, Annalaura hissed at Lottie with lips moving as little as she could manage.

"Quit those weeds, and come over here slow." Annalaura's whispered, no-nonsense command caught the girl openmouthed.

Fright replaced surprise on the child's face as she instantly dropped her fresh-pulled weed, bent double, and walk-ran to her mother. Annalaura's eyes remained on the horse and rider.

The visitor could only be a white man because no colored would be out riding the lanes when it was harvest time. Besides, no colored could afford a horse like the gray Annalaura saw approaching her. Dread as heavy as the Tennessee heat landed on her bare head. With her hands on the shoulders of both Henry and Lottie, she pushed them further behind her skirt. Without moving her head, she slid her eyes from side to side in a frantic attempt to locate Doug and Cleveland. She thought she spotted swaying in the tobacco stalks some fifteen rows distant. She prayed that both her boys would stay quiet and out of sight. Just before the rider slowed his horse enough to see her face, Annalaura dropped her eyes to a spot at the middle bricks of the smoke house. As the man reined in the gray some twenty yards from where she stood with the two children, she shifted her eyes to the horse's foreleg.

"You doin' any good out there?" Already, the voice was harsh and accusing her of the worst.

Just as she feared, the rider was the owner of the acres her family tenant farmed—Alexander McNaughton. She gave Henry and Lottie securing pats as she raised her head in line with the horse's flank. It was a carefully practiced motion that let her lift her eyes up to the rider's trunk so she could, at least, read his body movements with him unaware that she was watching.

"I'm doing right fine, suh." She kept her voice low with just the right amount of practiced servility in it. She saw McNaughton's brown-booted foot, covered by his faded work pants, stiffen in the saddle. She gauged him looking over the acres. She kept her neck bent and her eyes busy as she waited minutes for him to speak again.

"Don't look right fine to me." The suspicion in his voice came as no surprise to Annalaura.

She stilled her shaking shoulders. It was now her job to tell this white man that summer sun couldn't stop a determined colored woman from doing what she had to do, man or no man.

"Yas, suh." She made sure he heard the contriteness in her voice that she had been found out in a little white lie. "We's workin' hard at it, suh." She drew out his title in one long bowing-and-scraping breath. "Gonna bring it in for you, suh. Just like last year."

There. She had opened her battle plan. Remind him of the bumper crop her family had given him at the last harvest.

"Last year ain't this year, now is it, woman?" He shot her his first warning.

But, warning or no, Annalaura had too much to lose not to fight back.

"No, suh. It surely ain't."

McNaughton twisted in the saddle to scan the acres on the other side of the smoke house. She took the opportunity to raise her eyes a fraction of an inch while she still kept her neck bent low. When she watched the middle of his blue work shirt swivel back around in her direction, she saw his trunk incline slightly in the saddle toward her.

"These shoots ain't nowhere near tall enough." He let the accusation hang in the air for her ears to take in.

She knew this was not the time to answer. Suddenly, McNaughton's face came within line of her lowered vision as he bent over in the saddle to rest a forearm on his knee. Her racing heart picked up a pace, and she squeezed Henry and Lottie's faces into the folds of her hiked-up skirt. Little Henry coughed and she eased up just enough so the child could breathe. This white man was staring at her and her children.

"Those the only pickaninnies you got with you?" The words coming out of McNaughton's mouth lacked the same bite as the earlier ones, and to white ears, may have been heard as soothing.

But not to Annalaura. Without calculating the impact of her every word, she lifted her chin, and for a brief instant, looked directly into this white man's face. Her own inside warning system pounded through her ears, but her words came out faster than she could listen.

"I have four children, sir." Even though talking proper to a white man could earn her a good beating for being "uppity," she made sure he heard every syllable of her carefully enunciated sentence. She let every bit of the teaching she had received that one winter from the colored teacher down from Fisk University linger in each word. Her children deserved to hear from their momma's own lips that they were more than a white man's insults.

She dropped her eyes to just above McNaughton's belt buckle praying that he hadn't caught her twin infractions—raising her eyes to his face and speaking like colored could be educated the same as whites. She watched him sit upright in the saddle as his left hand jerked on the reins. Then he slid his forearm to his knee again. Barely aware, Annalaura dug her fingers hard into Lottie's shoulder as she fought not to look into this man's face a second time. She heard little Lottie's soft whimper of pain, and Annalaura began rubbing the sore spot.

"Tell me then, woman, where are your other two children?" His words and his sound didn't match, and Annalaura had to catch herself from looking directly at him.

He had called her a "woman." Coming out of the mouth of a white man addressing a black female, the word meant little more than hussy or worse—a woman ready to be led to a man's bed. If that's what he thought, she had to make quick amends. But the sound of him had suddenly softened, and that worried Annalaura even more.

"My older boys is workin' the far field, suh. One is almost fo'teen and the other jest about twelve." She knew the Lord would forgive her the lie.

With the greatest care, she eased her head up so she could see McNaughton's mouth. He was pursing his lips like he was thinking over some weighty issue.

"That would make 'em big enough to do some work." His tone sounded promising.

Annalaura couldn't help letting her eyes flash on his whole face. The top half of his head was shaded by his wide-brimmed straw hat, which kept her from reading his eyes. The lower half of his face was not as red from the sun as she expected. He turned his head slightly, and the light caught his deep blue eyes fixed on her.

With dawning horror, Annalaura realized that McNaughton had locked his eyes onto her bare legs. Thoughts tumbled in her head as her hands spasmodically opened and closed on the shoulders of her children. She wanted to loosen the knot at her middle and drop her hem to the ground. But nothing in God's Tennessee would allow her that modesty. No colored woman could ever show a white man that she believed he could be thinking those kinds of thoughts about a field hand. The heat and the worry made her head go light, and she felt herself sway.

"Ain't your man John Welles?" McNaughton eased the horse to the edge of the tobacco rows.

More to keep herself from falling, Annalaura's head came up. She fixed her eyes on his shoulders hoping that her offense would not be too great. Though she tried, her dry throat would not let her answer.

"Or do you have a man at all?" He didn't bother hiding the smirk in his voice.

She sensed his eyes scanning her thighs. One hand slipped from Henry's shoulder and almost went to the tie at her middle. She willed it back in place.

"Yas, suh. My husband is John Welles. He's gone up to Hopkinsville to see 'bout his folks. They doin' better now. My John should be back just about any hour now." She knew better than to ramble on like this with white folks, man or woman, but she had to let this man know that she was not an unattached colored woman. A colored woman without a man was fair game for every white man in Montgomery County.

"Hopkinsville is it?" McNaughton straightened in the saddle.

Annalaura kept her eyes on his shirt.

"What's Welles doin' in Hopkinsville?"

That he was about to catch her in a trap was draped over every word he uttered. McNaughton would want to know why John had taken off for Kentucky when he had forty acres of white man's tobacco to harvest in the next two weeks. Annalaura dropped her head lower. Hitched up skirt or no, she had to let him think that her husband knew his duty to white folks, to his family, and to his wife.

"My husband's family ain't from around here. They is from Kentucky. His auntie took bad off sick, but sick or well, my husband will be back to get in your tobacco." She jerked her head up quickly to indicate the acres in back of her.

She gave his face a quick read before she dropped her eyes again. He laid his forearm on his knee. With her eyes lifted as far as the lower half of his face, she watched him drop his head to the tops of her boots as he slowly slid his stare up her legs. She sensed his eyes come to rest just under the knot tied at her middle. A rash of prickly heat raised up on her lower abdomen.

"Woman, Hopkinsville or no, husband or no, you've got two weeks to get me my tobacco." She watched him straighten in the saddle. He pulled on the reins and headed the horse back up the path toward the lane. "Remember. Two weeks. 'Til the first of September, or you and your get are off this place."

She watched him dig his heels into the horse's side and set the animal trotting up the path and away from her.

CHAPTER FOUR

With little guidance from Alexander, the gray trotted up the path and turned right onto the lane bisecting his acres. He let the horse have his head as he fought the urge to look back. He didn't need a second glance to tell him what he already knew about the mid-forty. The tobacco stalks were too short, and he was middling uncertain if they could be brought in on time even if the woman did have a man on the place. He knew as well as she that the tobacco had to be in no later than mid-September, and that meant cut, stacked, and hung in the barn to dry. He hadn't dared hope that Welles could duplicate last year's profits, but getting nothing when he had hoped for at least fifteen hundred dollars would definitely be a blow. Determined as she was, that slip of a woman couldn't do the job, not even with the two older boys she'd lied about. No, it wasn't the tobacco that made him yearn to turn his head for one more look.

Rocking in the saddle as the gray moved down the two-buggy-wide lane to his back-forty, Alex let his mind wander to the woman. She didn't look like a good wind could blow her over, but neither was she built for work like most field hands. Eula had her beat by far in the husky department. Yet, he could see that she wasn't soft. One look at those tight, coppery-bronze thighs glistening in the mid-morning sun told him that. The way the rays caught the color of those bare legs made his mind wonder what other pleasures she had under that hiked-up dress.

Alex slowed the horse to a walk as the gray approached a leafy canopy of alders. This close to noon, they both needed a cooldown. He ran his shirtsleeve across his forehead trying to dismiss the growing pressure in his groin. McNaughton forced his thoughts onto the new family on the back-forty. What there was of tobacco on their plot was taller than the Welles's acres. But that family was never going to earn him three thousand dollars. He supposed they put their backs into the work, but they were not John Welles. As the gray continued its loping pace, Alex squirmed in the saddle. He couldn't keep the thoughts away. He remembered the first time he had seen the Welles woman.

Most of the tenant families looking to farm came in the fall to see if they could work the last few weeks of the harvest, hoping that the owner would then feed and shelter them all winter. He should have known then that there was something different about John Welles. The man had tapped on his back door in April, just at the time when the hard winter ground was breaking up and the best farmers wanted to start their plowing. Most tenants didn't want to work then. White man had to drive them to the fields, but not so for John Welles.

There the nigger stood, hat in hand, big and strapping, looking like he could do the job. Welles had done most of the talking with his woman and children standing behind him. Alex had to concede that John Welles had been as smooth as corn silk with his words, saying all the things a tobacco farmer wanted to hear from a prospective tenant. Even then he thought Welles had sounded almost too good. Now, Alex realized that just as the new applicant came close to crossing the line into uppity, his woman spoke up and reeled him back. Today, he remembered his first look at the wife.

Those amber eyes, with their slight upward tilt, had come up just a fraction of an inch too much whenever she spoke. Her words came soft and low, just like they did today, but they always took the edge off whatever her husband had just said. As soon as she got her piece out, she stopped and let her man speak until he skirted close to the line again, and there she was, smoothing over his too-glib words.

Alex couldn't put his finger on what was so different about her. He hadn't thought her uncommonly pretty back then, but he hadn't yet stared at the soft oval curves of her face, nor those full lips that looked just right for a man to suck into his mouth. He hadn't taken in the whole look of her until today. Back then, it had been more in the way she stood erect behind her man. Even in that shapeless flour sack of a dress she'd worn, he could still guess at the outlines of her slender figure. The gray cleared the welcoming shade. Alex flicked the reins again as he spotted the next set of trees in the distance. It was getting harder and harder to ignore the stiffening in his pants. He took off his straw hat and fanned his face as he shifted in the saddle. Lord knows he couldn't remember the last time a hardening had come on unbidden with Eula. In their first year of marriage, he recalled hankering after her in that way. After she lost the baby, he supposed her interest in him waned, and so did his in her. It wasn't that he didn't need a woman, and most of the time, it was Eula he bedded. Unlike other men down at the back room of the Lawnover store, he had no need to complain about Eula not being willing. That was another way in which she was good. His Eula never refused him like some men said their wives did. Even Eula's brother, Ben Roy, had complained against his Fedora. Alex never had that sort of trouble with Eula. As far as he could tell, she seemed all right with whatever he wanted. Come to think of it, she never troubled him by what she might have wanted or not wanted. She knew as well as he, that a woman was there to do a man's bidding in the bedroom, and the timing was his call. After twenty years of marriage, he only needed to come to her every two weeks. Of course, that didn't mean a man didn't need some variety every now and again.

An oriole swept down from the upper branches of an oak tree and swooped in front of the gray's eyes. The horse broke stride a second before Alex could steady it as horse and rider cleared the second stand of trees. Now that he'd seen her again, he guessed that the Welles woman had never gone all the way from his mind. No wonder. Blackberry juice kept a man young. Every white man in Montgomery County knew that.

Scrunching his brow, Alex reckoned that the last nigger woman he'd bedded was about six months back. He'd gotten to her first after he learned that her husband had been killed on the railroad down in Nashville. She'd been good for a few rounds, and like always, he knew the change would keep him faithful to Eula. It had never crossed his mind to be unfaithful to his wife. Unlike his Thornton in-laws, he didn't keep going back to the same nigger women year after year. Once or twice a year with a new woman each time was good enough for him.

Alexander rounded the slight bend in the lane and spotted the fence with the missing rail that separated his back-forty from the Thornton place. He reminded himself to get after that new man to get it fixed as soon as harvest ended. As the horse neared the path leading to the old log-hewn cabin, he wondered if the Welles woman really had a husband who was coming back "any hour now." If she did, she was off-limits. No white man in these parts went with a nigger who had a man around the place. Made no economic sense. Husband was sure to get surly and slow down the work, wrecking things for both himself and the farm owner. It was smart business to only mess with nigger women who had no man around, like the widow woman he had last winter.

As his gray turned onto the narrow path and started toward the new family working in the field, the hardening in his pants rubbed against the saddle. McNaughton knew the truth of it and so did the Welles woman. No matter what she said, the sharecropper's wife, with those legs ready and more than able to straddle a man, had no full-time husband about the place.

Alex trotted up the lane to his own barn after riding his acres. What to do about the mid-forty still hung in his mind. He gauged the time at nearly three in the afternoon. The sun reigned at its August hottest with the sky showing no sign of rain in the foreseeable future. Without rain, there was small chance the stalks would grow much taller, even with all the weeding the Welles woman was doing. Patting down the gray, he resolved to give more thought to the mid-forty after he'd eaten the midday meal Eula was holding for him. He stopped at the pump at his closed-in back porch to wash his hands.

Stepping through the rear porch door into the kitchen, he barely nodded a greeting to Eula, who moved quickly to her feet as soon as he appeared. Except for the clear space in front of his chair, the kitchen table was cluttered with dozens of Mason jars, some empty, some capped, and others filled with peach preserves. Alex pulled out the mash from the Lawnover store he had visited after making his rounds and laid it on the table next to Eula's account journal.

His wife scurried to the stove and began ladling string beans and fried corn onto his plate. She topped it with two deep-fried pork chops and set the plate, mounded with his dinner, before him. He watched Eula move to the safe to pull out a fork just before he discovered its absence on the table. On her way back, she stopped at the stove to cut off a hunk of corn bread. As his wife bent over to lay his bread on the oilcloth, Alex caught the strong aroma of vinegar.

"You wash your hair?" He didn't bother to hide the touch of surprise in his voice as he ran the date through his head.

He slid his eyes toward the almanac calendar hanging on the inside of the open pantry door. Today was Friday, but was it that Friday? He spotted the galvanized bathing tub sitting on the floor of the pantry. Normally, it would hang from its hook on the back porch. Eula had washed her hair and bathed.

"Uh huh" was her only sound as she pushed aside her journal and set down her own plate.

Did she expect him to remember these things? Every other Friday he took Eula to bed. It was a routine that had worked well for them for nearly seven years. What was the cause of the washed hair he wondered? She only did that about four times a year. But he had no time to probe the whys of Eula's actions. He would be ready for her tonight.

A light knock on the back door caught a forkful of string beans on their way to his mouth. He gave Eula an accusatory look. She knew better than to have visitors come when he was eating his meal. With "I'm sorry" written across her face, Eula left her own plate untouched as she pushed open the kitchen screen door and walked across the porch to the back door. Whoever it was, Alex trusted Eula to get rid of them as fast as possible. He was surprised when she returned and stood over him without starting her own meal.

"Some colored man's at the door." Her voice sounded apologetic.

"What colored man?" Alex wanted to hear none of this. Couldn't Eula see that he had just started his dinner? It was her house, and she was responsible for keeping niggers or anybody else away who would disturb him.

Still, she stood.

"New to Lawnover. Says his name is Isaiah Harris." When Eula made no motion to sit, Alex put down his fork and stared at her.

"Wants to know if he can farm for you next year?" The tail end of her voice ended in a question.

The mid-forty, never entirely off his mind all day, flooded Alex's thoughts.

"It's harvest time. Lots of tenants want to work two or three weeks at harvest and then coast off me for the next six months." Alex pushed back from the table, though he did not stand. He ran the possibilities through his mind.

"Maybe he could help out on the mid-forty?" Eula did not meet his eyes when his face trained on hers.

"Can't this nigger come back tomorrow?" Annoyed at the disturbance, still Alex wasn't at all sure the mid-forty could wait until tomorrow.

Before Eula could bob her head yea or nay, Alex got to his feet, almost knocking over the chair. "I'll get this over with now."

The man who greeted him outside the porch door, stood with his head bowed, waiting respectfully for Alex to begin his greeting. Alex took his time looking over the fellow. At first glance, the man looked able enough. Almost as tall but not nearly as muscular as John Welles, this one verged on the skinny.

"What's that name again?" Alex estimated the fellow to be in his early thirties.

A man in his thirties was usually a decent worker, while young bucks in their twenties were nothing but trouble. Alex searched his farmyard for the man's family.

"It's Isaiah, suh. Isaiah Harris." The man busied his fingers turning the brim of his hat over in his hands.

The lane to Lawnover swept right by his barnyard, and there was no sign of Harris's wife or children. Alex shifted his weight and stared at the applicant.

"Well, Isaiah, how old are you?" Alex folded his arms over his chest in growing unease. A man in his thirties should be fairly settled in his ways. Where was his woman?

"I'm thirty-one, suh." Isaiah kept his eyes properly on the ground, and Alex liked the way he stooped his shoulders. John Welles had stood a little too tall for his own good.

"How many in your family?" Alex asked with Eula standing right behind him.

"Ain't got none, suh." The man kept his eyes on the bottom stoop of the step where Alex stood.

"Ain't got no what? Don't have no family or don't have no wife?" Alex's face drooped into a frown. "A man old as you ought to have a family unless he's a sportin' man. You a sportin' man, Isaiah?" He could smell the vinegar in Eula's hair assaulting his nose.

"Naw, suh. I ain't no sportin' man. Jest ain't got me enough money to get me a wife right now." Isaiah twirled the hat in his hands faster.

"How you gonna bring in forty acres of tobacco all by yourself?" Alex's frown deepened.

A single man most often brought a ruckus with him. Women helped settle a man—black or white. Something in his gut felt uneasy about the idea of an unmarried man on the mid-forty. Alex had just about made up his mind about Isaiah Harris when Eula whispered in his ear.

"He won't be by himself. That missing man's wife and her older boys can pitch in." The sound of her voice startled him and he half-turned toward her. "As soon as the crop is in, you can send them all on their way."

Though getting rid of a sharecropper who ran off whenever the notion took him felt like a good idea in Alex's head, Eula knew better than to bring up business matters to him, even if it was only in front of a nigger. He wondered if his wife had taken sick with her strange behavior.

"Isaiah, I'm goin' to think on it and let you know day after tomorrow. In the meantime, you think about gettin' yo'self a woman to keep you through the winter." He heard Eula gasp at his suggestion of unmarried cohabitation.

He smiled. Hell, they were just niggers. The Bible didn't say nothing about niggers not sleeping together before they were married. His mind flashed on Eula's brother, Ben Roy Thornton. What would the Bible say about him? Married to Fedora for almost twenty-five years, he'd kept the same nigger woman for almost six of them. As he closed the door on Isaiah, Alex decided that Ben Roy had committed no sin. After all, his brother-in-law wasn't keeping company with a white woman.

That night after Eula dried and put up the last of the supper dishes, he lay in bed waiting for her. When she slipped in beside him wearing her summer cotton nightshirt that covered her from neck to ankles, he turned off the lamp. No need to waste oil on seeing a sight that he had looked upon for twenty years. Though she had never had much in the way of curves and highs and lows, it was still better to remember her the way she used to be rather than the thick flabbiness he touched nowadays. Some Fridays he felt like he was laying his body across one of his downed alder trees after a spring flood. It was thoughts of the alone nigger woman on the mid-forty that hardened him enough to put it to Eula Mae this night.

CHAPTER FIVE

Though she never regretted her marriage to Alexander McNaughton and the stepped-down life it brought her, Eula still took great comfort standing in the oversize Thornton kitchen where her mother had directed the preparation of so many family meals. Back in Momma's time, one day during the last two weeks of August had always been set aside for the preserving and storing of the fruits of the garden and the arbor. Momma had a full-time colored cook and a cook's helper, but this special day was the time when all the Thornton women, blood and in-laws alike, gathered to peel, core, boil, and jar for the barren winter months. These days, there were about half a dozen more female Thornton kin than back in Momma's time. Still, the job took a whole day.

While Alex was off riding the fields, Eula had gotten up when it was still dark to gather and feed the chickens and hogs. She had milked all three cows before she readied herself to get into the buckboard Alex had hitched up for her. The ride to her childhood home on the neighboring farm had taken no longer than fifteen minutes.

Standing at the new six-eye, coal-burning stove Ben Roy had just bought for his Fedora, Eula alternated sampling from the five big iron kettles, all in various stages of cooking. She delighted in the routine of sameness, and through the years of this mass production had developed an efficient process to get the job done on the allotted day. Now, with six burners, she could keep five pots simmering, instead of three, with the sixth eye available for the cooling. That would cut off about three hours of sweat-pouring work. In the years since she took over the job as main canning-day cook from her dead mother, Eula had learned to block out the Thornton women's chatter and lose herself in her own memories of girlhood.

Although there were four Thornton sons, Eula and Bessie had been the only girls. She and her sister could not have been more dissimilar. Bessie, five years younger and half a head shorter, had taken more after their curvaceous mother in height and build, but she was her father's spitting image in coloring. Bessie's hair had definite yellows and light browns to it, while Alexander had once described Eula's hair color as "neither this nor that…more like the color of house dust…" Eula knew in her heart that he hadn't meant to hurt, so she never held the remark against him. But Old Ben had clearly favored his younger daughter with her creamy complexion, pinched-in waist, high bosom, and light brown eyes. Old Ben had said Eula's eyes reminded him of the burned underside of a cook pot. Her father had meant to hurt, and Eula did hold it against him.

Her father had just about cried when that Kentucky man came down and asked for Bessie's hand though she was only sixteen. It had taken Momma Thornton a lot of breath to convince her husband that the marriage would be a very profitable one for Bessie. But the old man had still been reluctant to bestow his blessings on the union until Momma reminded him that Eula would never make such a good marriage. In fact, their oldest daughter stood an excellent chance of being an old maid. In that case, it would be up to Bessie to take in her sister. Unable to deny the wisdom of his wife's reasoning, Old Ben bid a sorrowful good-bye to his favorite daughter.

"Eula Mae, are those peaches 'bout ready?" Cora Lee, one of the Thornton cousins, jarred Eula out of her musings as she stuffed a tea towel into a Mason jar to complete its drying.

Ignoring the annoying Cora Lee, Eula bent over a pot of dark cherries just coming to a boil. She lowered her long-handled wooden spoon into a second kettle on a back burner. Filling it only a quarter full and raising it to her lips, she blew on the hot peaches to cool them before she stuck out a tongue to sample.

"I declare, Aunt Eula, I don't know how you can stand there over all those cooking pots in this heat." Tillie, Ben Roy and Fedora's just-married twenty-one-year-old daughter, patted the kitchen table, which was nearly covered with bowls of cherries, pits, peaches, cored apples, plums, sugar, flour, glass jars, lids, and sealing wax. Tillie's hand came to rest on her aunt's account journal. Flipping to the back cover, the newlywed began to tear at the last page.

Without thinking, Eula tapped the wooden spoon on the edge of the iron pot holding the cherries.

"Tillie, your momma's got a fan in the kitchen safe. Use it, not one of my journal pages." Eula gave her niece an apologetic smile.

"Eula Mae, you still writin' down everything in that journal of yours? How many jars of this and how many cans of that? I declare, all that figurin' would drive me crazy." Fedora waved the paring knife in the air while she held a half-cored apple in the other hand. "I can't be bothered. I just use stuff 'til I run out. If I need more, Ben Roy will buy it off'n somebody." Finished with the cored apple, Fedora handed it over to Cora Lee.

With a few quick strokes of her butcher knife, Cora cubed the apple into six parts.

"I just like to know how much I have so I can pace myself." Eula really wanted to tell Fedora that her Thornton mother-in-law had insisted that the mark of a good homemaker was how well she kept her farm books.

Mother Thornton had been a master at managing the household accounts on the large farm, and while Bessie was the prime target of her instruction, Eula had been a keen observer.

Right after her sister left for Kentucky, Alexander came courting Eula, if courting was the right word. There had been no long buggy rides in the country, nor any chaperoned picnics under the elms with Alex. He sat with her one time at the church social and the next she knew, Old Ben told her that a McNaughton had asked for her hand. She really didn't need her mother's constant reminders of how lucky she was to have escaped spinsterhood, especially since her twenty-second birthday was just six months away. Eula needed no prodding. She knew she was fortunate that a good-looking man had wanted her. Though the McNaughtons were just a notch above piss-poor, Alexander was more mannerable than her brothers. Better still, she had quickly understood the rules of their marriage from the outset.

Her husband had needed a good manager for his farm, and she had provided that and more. It took her no time to anticipate his every need before the thought came into his head. Even when she knew his decisions were wrong-headed, like the time he bought a lame racehorse with most of their year's tobacco money only to have to destroy the animal four months later, Eula held her tongue and stretched the two months' worth of winter supplies into four. Since she never talked back to Alex, nor disobeyed his orders, he had never raised a hand against her like Eula was sure Ben Roy had done to Fedora. She would love Alexander McNaughton forever, no matter what might come between them, because he had shown her his tender side when he held her in his arms all night after their baby girl had been born dead.

If there had been any problems between herself and Alexander, Eula would never discuss them with Fedora, though Ben Roy's wife was the closest in age and sibling order to herself. Even though Fedora always did act more Thornton than the blood Thorntons, and commanded the other females to confide in her, Eula never dared chance that discussion. She admired her sister-in-law for many things, but she never liked to confront her on anything because the outspoken woman always had to have the last say.

"Eula, how 'bout those peaches?" Jenny, a cousin on Eula's father's side, asked as she took two dried Mason jars from Eula's young niece. "Tillie, get over there and check on your aunt and them peaches."

"Hey, Jenny," Fedora's sharp voice snapped through the kitchen. "You ought to know by now that Eula is the best cook in the Thornton family. Because she don't have a hired girl, she's got more practice than the rest of us put together." Fedora kept her eyes on the apple in her hand. "Them peaches will be ready when Eula says they are. If you want to get yo'self out of here before the chickens go to roost, we'd all better stick to our own jobs."

In some ways Fedora had the kind of manner that Eula envied. Her older brother's wife said what she thought when she thought it, and she never bothered to put a sugar coating on it. Eula remembered how pleased her father had been when Ben Roy announced, proud as a fightin' cock, that Fedora had agreed to marry him. The bride-elect had been fair-to-middling pretty with her straight, dark brown hair and eyes that slanted just a bit like an Indian's. Fedora was low to the ground, though you would never know it by the way she bossed every Thornton woman, and half the Thornton men. Ben Roy bragged on catching Fedora, but Eula always thought it should have been the other way around. Her brother, by himself, inherited half of their father's six hundred and forty acres.

"Tillie, take these apples on over to your aunt." Belle Thornton, wife of Eula's younger brother, Jessie Roy, commanded her niece.

Eula dipped the spoon back into the low-simmering pot of peaches for a second sampling. She held out the spoon to offer Tillie a taste only to see her niece's eyes grow wide and the recent bride's face blanch white. Grabbing at her stomach, Tillie turned and ran through the kitchen and disappeared beyond the dining room door.

"If you asked me," Belle slid the rubber seal around the necks of the Mason jars as they came at her in assembly-line fashion, "I'd say she's in a family way. Wasn't that wedding in June?"

Eula buried her gasp in the steaming pot of cubed apples. Cora cleared her throat. It didn't take long for Fedora to pounce.

"Are you counting the months since my girl's wedding, Belle Thornton?" Fedora's eyes flamed.

"I ain't sayin' nothing bad 'bout your Tillie." After fifteen years as a Thornton, Belle still hadn't learned not to bait Fedora. "I know it's been two months since she walked down the aisle in that tight-fittin' dress. All I'm saying is that it's about time for a baby."

"Don't you think I'd know if my own daughter was expectin'?" Fedora bristled.

Although the warmth from the stove and the smothering outside heat creeping through the open kitchen windows made her woozy, Eula bent her head closer to the steam from the cherry pot. As her own sweat dripped into the kettle, she could hear the other women squirm in their chairs.

"Maybe she don't know herself," Jenny interjected.

"That's right, I sure didn't know," answered Belle. "All that marryin' business is just so overpowerin' anyway. That first year, a woman don't know if she's comin' or goin'." Belle pounded the edge of her knife against the table.

Eula set her mouth in a firm line to stop the forming frown. On the morning of her wedding, she had fidgeted while Mother Thornton instructed her on the ways of the wedding night. "He's a man," Momma had said. "Let him have his way with nary a complaint nor a whine. You just lay there and it'll be over quick. Whatever you do, don't give him no encouragement."

Abruptly, Eula dropped her wooden spoon into the pot of just-put-on plums and walked over to the kitchen table to retrieve her journal. Pulling a pencil from her apron pocket, she picked up her account book and neatly marked a three besides the peaches column and a four next to the column lettered "cherries." Belle, Jenny, and Cora gave her only cursory glances while Fedora continued with the apple coring. Tillie slowly made her way back into the room, her face showing dampness from the water she must have splashed over it.

"I saw yo' husband, Wiley George, at the Lawnover store the other day," Jenny spoke out as Eula slipped her journal back to the table and made her way over to the stove. "He looked like a happy bridegroom to me."

"Tillie, when did you last have your rags washed out?" Fedora plunged the paring knife deep into a half-cored apple.

"Momma." She whispered in a voice heard by every woman in the room.

"I checked your rags myself about two weeks before you married Wiley George." Fedora frowned as though her mind was clicking off the months. "That was back in the first part of June. Well, have you dirtied any rags since then?"

"Momma" was all Tillie managed a second time.

"Fedora, it's as plain as the nose on your face that she's expectin'." Belle announced airily.

"Tillie, get over here." Fedora rose to her feet as Tillie made her way slowly around the table toward her mother. As the girl approached, Fedora laid her hand across her daughter's belly and leaned an ear close. Sitting back down, Fedora looked right past Cora and turned to Eula.

"It's a baby all right," Fedora announced as Cora nodded her head.

"A baby? Momma, I can't have no baby. Not now. I just got married." Tillie's voice held the distinct sound of encroaching hysteria.

"Fedora, didn't you tell this girl where babies come from?" Belle could barely eke out the words through her laughter.

At the stove, Eula turned her back to the women. Suddenly, the steam from the pots and the hundred-degree kitchen heat almost overwhelmed her. She leaned against the handle on the oven door. Closing her eyes, Eula tried to steel herself against more talk of babies.

"Momma, I could die givin' birth." Tillie sank into a vacant chair.

"It's nineteen-thirteen, missy, and I reckon old Doc Starter knows enough to get that baby safe out of you." Fedora, like mothers before her, dismissed Tillie's fears.

"And you can't use that excuse to get out of your duty to Wiley George, neither." Cora Lee snickered.

"Every woman here knows about a wife's duty to her husband, Cora Lee." Fedora had just about reached her own boiling point. "We don't need you to remind us."

Eula's own pregnancy had started off like Tillie's with sometime sickness in the mornings, but that had been slight and she had worked the farm alongside Alex. As for her wifely duties, despite what her mother had said, after the first few times, she hadn't minded at all. Through the years, if she let herself, she found her duties downright enjoyable. It was becoming increasingly harder to follow her mother's advice and "just lay there." Many a night, especially now that Alex was only coming to her every other Friday, she wanted to put her arms around his neck and run her hands down his back. Sometimes she wanted to push him so deep inside her that he would have to fight to catch his breath for love of her. But if she did any of those things, he would think she was an easy woman just as her mother predicted. "It's the way of a husband. Don't act like you enjoy it. He'll think you learned those things from some other man." Eula often wondered what "those things" were and how did her mother know about them, anyway?

"You are as strong as an ox, Tillie Thornton Jamison," Fedora pronounced. "You will have this baby and keep Wiley George happy too.